The
Problem
with
Chickens

by
Bruce McMillan

illustrated with paintings by
Gunnella

Houghton Mifflin Company

Boston

Walter Lorraine Books

More information about the author can be found at www.brucemcmillan.com.
More information about the illustrator can be found at www.gunnella.info.

The oil paintings were done using Winsor & Newton Winton Oil Colours and Winsor & Newton Short Flat Galleria brushes on Fredrix Standard Red Label prestretched canvas, and covered with Winsor & Newton Retouching Varnish.

Walter Lorraine ⟨wℓ⟩ Books

Text copyright © 2005 by Bruce McMillan
Illustrations copyright © 2005 by Gudrun Elin Olafsdottir

www.houghtonmifflinbooks.com

Library of Congress Cataloging-in-Publication Data

McMillan, Bruce.
  The problem with chickens / by Bruce McMillan; illustrated with paintings by Gunnella.
    p. cm.
  "Walter Lorraine books."
  Summary: When women in an Icelandic village buy chickens to lay eggs for them to use, the chickens follow them, adopting human ways and forgetting their barnyard roots, until the ladies hatch a clever plan.
  ISBN-13: 978-0-618-58581-6 (hardcover)
  ISBN-10: 0-618-58581-8 (hardcover)
[1. Chickens—Fiction. 2. Iceland—Fiction.] I. Gunnella, ill. II. Title.

PZ7.M47878Pro 2005
[E]—dc22

                                                      2005001225

Manufactured in China
SCP 10 9 8 7 6 5 4 3 2

Designed by Bruce McMillan
The text is set in 20-point Cochin.

In a small village on the far end of Iceland there were plenty of eggs, even if there were no chickens.

The eggs were on the cliffs where the wild birds lived. There were more eggs here than the ladies of the village could ever use for cooking.

But it was too difficult for the ladies to get these eggs. Their husbands might have gathered them, but the men were always too busy fishing and farming.

So the ladies traveled to the city to buy some chickens.

The chickens were happy in the village. Every day they laid many eggs. The ladies were overjoyed to have so many eggs for cooking. Their cakes were delicious. That is when the problem started.

The chickens forgot they were chickens. They started acting like ladies.

When the ladies went to pick blueberries, the chickens went too.

When the ladies went to a birthday party, the chickens went too.

When the ladies sang to the sheep, the chickens sang too.

When the ladies took a rest from their gardening, the chickens rested too.

Everything the ladies did, the chickens did too.

The ladies couldn't even have tea and cakes by themselves.

The chickens were so
busy acting like ladies
that one day they stopped
laying eggs.

That's when the ladies said, "We have a problem."

So the ladies came up with an idea. It was a very clever idea. They would fool the chickens.

The ladies started exercising.

Soon the chickens, just like the ladies, were exercising.

Day after day the chickens exercised, just like the ladies.

Their wings grew stronger and stronger.

Then the ladies lifted the chickens, one by one, into the air and said, "Remember, you are birds."

The chickens flew to places on the cliffs where no other Icelandic birds lived. There they made their nests and laid their eggs.

This could have been a problem, but the ladies had planned for
this.

The chickens weren't the only ones who got strong from all that exercise.

Finally, the strong chickens in the far end of Iceland acted like birds.

And the strong Icelandic ladies had no problem gathering the eggs.

Also, from then on . . .

. . . if the ladies ever needed to go to the city . . .

...it was no problem at all.